ultra sports

marathon skiing

by Sandy Stiefer

the rosen publishing group's
rosen
central

For Dave, whose delightful face plant over
twenty years ago can still make me laugh

Published in 2002 by The Rosen Publishing Group, Inc.
29 East 21st Street, New York, NY 10010

First Edition

Library of Congress Cataloging-in-Publication Data

Stiefer, Sandy.
Marathon skiing / by Sandy Stiefer.
p. cm. — (Ultra sports)
Includes bibliographical references and index.
Summary: An exploration of cross-country skiing, including the history of the sport, profiles of top skiers, and beginners' tips on training, safety, gear, and types of events.
ISBN 0-8239-3554-X (lib. bdg.)
1. Cross-country skiing—Juvenile literature. [1. Cross-country skiing.]
I. Title. II. Series.
GV855.35 .S74 2002
796.93'2—dc21

2001004953

Manufactured in the United States of America

contents

Introduction: Feel the Burn
5

1
In the Beginning
10

2
Beginning the Burn
17

3
Ski Safety
24

4
Cross-Country Gear
30

5
Ultra Techniques
38

6
Competitive Racing
44

52   Glossary
54   Ultra Info
58   Ultra Reading
61   Index

What are ultra sports? Ultra sports emphasize endurance, doing an activity for a long time and over a great distance. In order to be tops in an ultra sport you need to be in excellent physical condition.

Marathon skiing is cross-country skiing over a great distance and for a long time. It involves pushing yourself to ultra fitness, ultra performance, and ultra endurance. Cross-country, or XC, is a supremely aerobic sport, so even if you're just out practicing it can feel like you're skiing a marathon.

Cross-country skiing has a long history. People in snowy climates were skiing long before bikes, cars, inline skates, and scooters were around. As other forms of snow transportation, such as snow-mobiles, snowplows, snow tires, and four-wheel drive vehicles were invented, people continued to ski for fun.

Cross-Country vs. Downhill

Since skiing takes many forms, let's first clarify what XC is and isn't. Cross-country skiing is also known as Nordic skiing. Nordic skiing, the granddaddy of all ski sports, is actually a group of ski techniques, styles, and events that have their origins in Scandinavia. In Nordic skiing, the heel of the boot is not attached to the ski. In this way, cross-country skiers can move their feet and legs in a gliding motion and propel themselves across fields of snow.

Downhill, or Alpine skiing, developed as an offshoot of Nordic skiing. Downhill skiing is just that—you take a chair lift up a mountain, then ski downhill. Alpine ski boots are fully attached to downhill skis. This gives Alpine skiers better turning ability for the higher speeds at which they ski.

Cross-country skiing activities can range from fun and easy glides across snow-covered golf courses or ski parks to races and marathons. Cross-country skiing can take place on ground that is as flat as a tortilla or down the same slopes used by Alpine skiers and snowboarders.

Competitors racing in cross-country relay at the Nordic Ski World Championship in Lahti, Finland.

Classic and Freestyle

There are two styles of cross-country skiing: classic and freestyle. Classic cross-country is also called traditional, or diagonal skiing. Classic cross-country devotees use a straight-ahead gliding motion, usually in prepared tracks made by skiers at a resort or club area. You can also cross-country ski in powder (deep snow)—you just won't set any speed records.

Freestyle cross-country skiing is also called ski skating. Skiers push their legs from side to side, much like skaters. They push off with their poles at the same time to gain more speed or power to get up hills. Ski skaters typically use trails that have groomed skating lanes. But ski skaters can also do it on any hard-packed snow. Cross-country and marathon ski races can involve either classic or freestyle skiing. Both usually take place on groomed trails.

Classic XC skis are skinny, with a long, curved front that is pointed. Both freestyle and classic XC skiers use what are called skinny skis. At first glance, you may wonder how you can get from point A to point B on such a pair of toothpicks. Many Alpine skiers used to view XC gear as rather simple, boring, and low tech. But cross-country gear has changed over the past several years. It has become as fashionable and high tech as any other sports gear.

Marathon Skiing

A marathon is a long race. It's an endurance contest. During a marathon, you might ski up to fifty-five kilometers in one day. Cross-country ski marathons involve almost every muscle in the body. Marathon skiers seek ultra fitness and like to push their bodies as

The biathlon (cross-country skiing and rifle marksmanship) and ski jumping (*left*) are two other kinds of competitive Nordic events.

hard as they can. They want to compete and test just how well they have trained. They like bringing it all together—fitness, equipment, and technique.

Only an endurance athlete skis marathons. Burning muscles and pumping lungs are part of ultra performance. Pain comes from pushing your body to the highest level of performance it can muster; to the dedicated marathon skier, this ultra pain hurts so bad it feels good.

There are a number of marathon ski competitions throughout the world, including the United States and Canada. Nordic ski events are also part of the Olympics. The United States didn't make a strong showing in international competition until 1976. That year, American XC skier Bill Koch won an Olympic medal in the sport. The popularity of cross-country skiing then soared. Many people from coast to coast began to cross-country ski. In the 1980s, however, as the interest in downhill skiing and extreme sports rose, interest in cross-country skiing fell.

Today, enthusiasm for cross-country skiing is on the rise. Now the clothes and gear are high tech and totally cool. Lots of everyday people cross-country ski. And many athletes who want to test themselves find racing and marathon skiing an ultra challenge.

When it comes to cross-country skiing, you can be as ultra as you want to be. You can enjoy XC right in your own backyard or at the nearest golf course. These choices avoid expensive lift tickets and long waiting lines associated with downhill skiing. Whether you go for the easy glide or for the burn of the marathon, you'll have fun in this ultra sport.

In the Beginning

People began cross-country skiing over 4,000 years ago in the northern European region now known as Scandinavia. Scandinavia is composed of three countries: Norway, Sweden, and Denmark. Rock carvings in Roday, Norway, show a person standing on skis and holding a hunting tool. These petroglyphs date from 2500 BC. Sweden owns the earliest known skis. They are more than 4,000 years old.

The countries of Scandinavia rest far north of the equator, so they have very cold climates and a great deal of snow. Ancient Scandinavians needed a way to get around in all of that snow. They figured out that if they strapped some flat branches or long animal bones to their feet, they could travel across the snow faster than by walking.

The first skis were pretty crude. The early Scandinavians used branches to hold the skier's feet onto the ski. Later, they used thick pieces of wood from the pine forests near which they lived. The first skis were heavy, having been cut from a single piece of wood and measuring anywhere from eight to fifteen feet long. Early skiers didn't use poles but many carried spears for hunting. They soon began to use their spears to make skiing up hills easier and for steering when skiing down hills.

One of the most famous stories in the history of cross-country skiing is that of the fierce Norwegian warriors called the Birkebeiners. These warriors wore leggings made from the bark of birch trees in order to keep snow out of their moccasins (soft leather shoes). The Birkebeiners guarded the king of Norway during the Norwegian Civil War of 1140–1210. They skied the king's son from Lillehammer to the safety of Reva, fifty-five kilometers away. When he grew up he became King Hakon Hakonsson IV. Today, Birkebeiner ski races are held to honor the prince's rescue. Norway, Canada, and the United States hold Birkebeiner races each year.

Cross-Country Comes to America

Some historians believe that Leif Erickson and other Vikings brought cross-country skiing to North America about 900 years ago. They landed in what is now Greenland and Canada. They would have needed XC skis to get around in the harsh winter snows. We do know that Scandinavian immigrants introduced skiing to the American Midwest and to California during the gold rush of the 1840s. The skis they used were twenty feet long—in fact, they were longer than those used in Scandinavia. Mine workers used skis to get to work and also to have a little fun. They had races and flew down hills on those heavy, thick skis.

Skiing Gets a Lift

Beginning in the 1930s, skiing gear and techniques went through many changes. Many people began to ski, and ski schools were opened. In 1932 the Union Pacific Railroad Company built the Sun Valley, Idaho, ski resort. They also built ski lifts. This invention had a major impact on the skiing world. The ski lift carried skiers to the tops of tall mountains, relieving people of long, hard climbs.

The advent of the chairlift created a new type of skiing that came to be known as Alpine (mountain). Many former cross-country skiers only liked going downhill and wanted to avoid the endurance aspect of skiing across the countryside. The ski lift let them ski how they liked best—speeding downhill!

Ancient Snowshoes

Twentieth-century scientists dug up a pair of what were first thought to be skis, but were later determined to be snowshoes, in Siberia, a region in northern Russia. They dated back to 2500 BC and were made of woven reeds.

Alpine slopes that have ski lifts, such as Geilo in Norway, can also be used for telemarking.

Telemarking combines downhill skiing with XC. Telemarkers ski on Alpine slopes served by lifts. Telemarking is done by linking turns. In the turn, one ski is forward while the other is back. The skier appears to be kneeling, but is actually using his or her legs for balance and control. By pressing the inside edge of the lead ski into the snow, the skier moves in a curve, back and forth down the slope. As the sport of Alpine skiing grew, with its specialized gear such as the fixed-heel boot, telemarking fell out of favor. But in recent years it has become popular again.

The Skiing Mailman

John Thorensen, a Norwegian immigrant, who became known as Snowshoe Thompson, was the first skiing mailman in the Unites States. He skied on twenty-five-pound boards and carried his heavy pack for twenty years (1856–1876), delivering the mail across the Sierra Nevada Mountains that border California and Nevada.

Competitions

As skiing is an activity with 4,000 years of history, there's no telling just when the first cross-country race was held. The first documented organized cross-country race was held in northern Norway in 1843. In 1904, after a race in Ishpeming, Michigan, the National Ski Association of America was formed by a group of Norwegian ski leaders. Soon thereafter, ski clubs began forming all around the United States. As more clubs formed, more races were held.

Today, countries around the world host XC race loppets. Loppets are ski races for nonprofessionals. They are events that bring young and old together for a long XC ski event. People race against themselves, not just others in the loppet. After the

A German cross-country skier approaches the finish line at the 1936 Winter Olympics in Germany.

race, a feast is usually held to celebrate the day. There are a number of these races throughout Scandinavia. Almost every community has its own. The Birkebeiner annual loppet in Norway is fifty kilometers long and commemorates Prince Hakon Hakonsson being skied to safety during the Norwegian War. Scandinavians brought loppets to North America and many other parts of the world.

For the real competitor, there are annual international races such as the World Cup, Junior World Championships, Nordic

Bill Koch

Bill Koch, a native of Vermont, started skiing when he was three years old. He skied to and from school. He went on to become one of the best XC skiers in the world. Cross-country skiing in the United States wasn't especially popular before the 1970s. It caught on after Americans began to compete successfully in international ski racing. Bill Koch was the first American Olympic cross-country victor in 1976 when he won the silver medal in the 30-kilometer race at Innsbruck, Austria. He also won the 1982 World Cup in cross-country skiing. With this contribution, in 1982 the United States had the fourth-best men's team in the world. Koch also made marathon skating, a cross-country technique used for racing on the flats and gradual uphills, popular.

World Ski Championships, and the Loppet World Cup. Of course, XC skiing has been part of the Olympics since the first Winter Olympiad in 1924.

Just about anyone can cross-country ski. Even those who are disabled participate in ski events and competitions. If you're not up to becoming an endurance athlete (though you might surprise yourself once you get started!), don't sweat it. Just ski for the fun of it!

Kids, teens, adults, and seniors can cross-country ski, as well as compete. The motions of XC are similar to striding and swinging your arms when walking briskly. This rhythmic opposite-leg-opposite-arm motion gives XC a natural feeling. Since XC is easy to learn and the injury rate is low, millions enjoy it.

While many XC skiers do like to push themselves to the limit, you can have a fun, easy glide through a park or golf course. The best thing about XC is that if you live in a snowy climate,

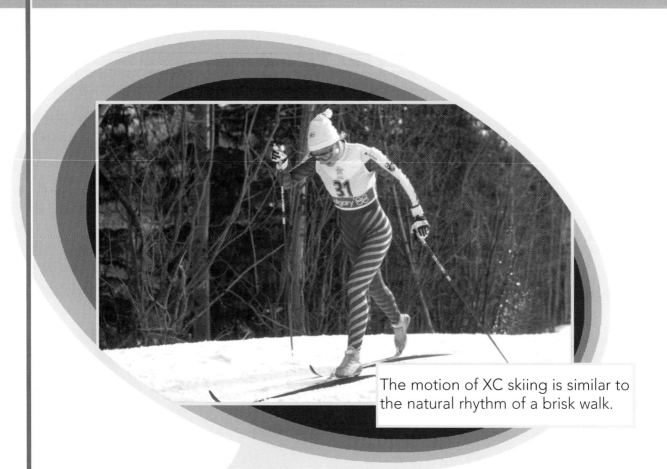

The motion of XC skiing is similar to the natural rhythm of a brisk walk.

you can easily strap on the boards and glide down the sidewalk or across a few backyards (better ask first!). But if you want to build your skills and have more thrills, you'll probably want to find a ski park or resort. There, you'll be able to ski a variety of terrain and learn more techniques. And you may just decide to try a race or two.

Taking Lessons

Since the classic XC technique is fairly easy to learn, you can pick up the basic movement pretty quickly. If you have friends who ski, they can help you practice. But if you want to learn new techniques and build your skills, you'll want to take lessons from a professional instructor.

Ski Talk

Boards: Skis.

Bodygroom: Falling so that your whole body gets covered in snow.

Face plant: Falling on your face in the snow.

Lifts: In Alpine skiing, the chairs you ride to the top of a mountain.

Pole plant: Using ski poles for balance or pushing off.

Shuffle: A walking motion during which you scuff your feet, not lifting them far off the ground.

Skinny skis: Another name for XC skis.

A ski instructor can also show you the safest way to fall. Every skier falls; that's a fact of standing on slim boards and slippery snow. Lessons will help you avoid some face plants and give you an opportunity to practice skiing up and down hills safely.

If you are interested in taking ski lessons, you might check your phone book. Look under "ski" or "ski resorts." Looking under "ski equipment" might also lead you to a ski shop. Someone there

Take Your Dog!

Dogs like to ski, too! In fact, the activity of skiing with dogs is known as *skijouring*. Skijouring is Norwegian for "ski-driving." A skier and his or her dog(s) wear a special racing harness. The dog's harness connects to the skier's at the waist, enabling the dog to pull the skier. Skijour races are often held in conjunction with sled-dog races.

What about stopping the dogs? It's all in the voice. "Whoa!" works just fine. You should be a pretty good skier before you try skijouring, though. You may also need to get permission to skijour on trails since dogs can mess up groomed trails in many ways.

might be able to help you find a school or an instructor. And don't forget to ask friends and acquaintances. If they ski they might already know of teaching organizations. Try to get your training from a PSIA (Professional Ski Instructors of America) or CANSI (Canadian Association of Nordic Ski Instructors) professional.

Equipment Basics

To get started you'll need the basics: skis with boot bindings that fit you, poles, and boots. Basic XC boot bindings have plastic or metal teeth and look like a horseshoe. The special boot has a sole that sticks out beyond the shoe toe. The horseshoe clamp holds the toe in place while allowing the heel to be raised.

Most cross-country skis need waxing—meaning you must wax the bottoms according to the type of snow and the weather conditions you will be skiing in. You can get beginner classic skis that are waxless so you don't have to deal with learning all about waxing right away. Waxless skis are a little slower than skis that have been waxed, but beginners won't notice the difference.

Winter sports require winter clothes. You don't have to invest in expensive ski clothes to XC ski. Some people ski in jeans, but they can limit your movement. Jeans become wet from the snow, too, and then you can grow cold. You'll have more ease of movement if you wear something that doesn't bind you.

Renting Equipment

If you live within a few hours drive from a major ski area, you may be able to rent gear and take it with you to the ski area. You can also rent equipment at the ski resort. But if there is a

Skiers try on ski boots inside a ski shop. It is important to get boots and poles that fit.

heavy skier turnout on a particular weekend, you may arrive at the resort only to find that all of the equipment has been rented to other skiers. Call ahead and check on rentals before you leave home.

It's tempting to become gung ho about a sport. You'll be tempted to run out and buy a bunch of gear and then head for the action. But it's important to rent skis for your first couple of tries. This way you can get a feeling for the sport and for various equipment. If you get hooked on cross-country skiing, as many people do, then you'll find out more about what kind of gear you need.

Where to Ski

You can ski at resorts or ski centers. Also, most states have bike trails that are used for walking, skiing, and snowmobiling during the winter months. While these trails may not offer groomed ski tracks,

A cross-country skier skis in Mercer County Park in West Windsor, New Jersey.

you will certainly be able to ski there. You can make tracks on the way in and then use those smooth tracks on the way out. Skating, or freestyle XC, may be a bit difficult without a groomed trail. Get in touch with your local chamber of commerce or park system to find out about trails.

You might also think about joining a club, as there are many Nordic ski clubs across the nation. There may be one where you live. Many schools, especially high schools, have ski clubs that hold various ski activities, including trips to XC parks or resorts. A club is a great place to make friends who share your interest. It's also a great place for beginners to learn more about skiing.

Ski Safety

Injuries are pretty rare for cross-country skiers who ski on groomed trails. About the worst that might happen is a face-first fall into the snow. But since you never know what might be hidden beneath the snow, it's best to try to ski under control and maintain your balance.

It is also important to remember that weather conditions can change quickly. Sudden storms can surprise an unprepared skier miles out from a ski resort or touring center.

The risk of injury increases if you love to ski in rugged backcountry. The risk of avalanches is ever present if you're skiing off prepared trails.

In order to keep yourself safe, learn all you can about skiing, winter weather, first aid, and survival. Taking lessons

Because weather conditions can change quickly, new skiers should stay close to resorts or touring centers.

from a PSIA or CANSI professional instructor will help you learn what you need to know. Your instructor can refer you to other organizations that offer classes, such as first-aid classes offered by the Red Cross.

Check Yourself and Equipment

While just about anyone can cross-country ski, if you've been a couch dweller for the past year it's a good idea to have a sports physical. If you rent equipment it should be in good working condition. Always double check. Check the bindings to be sure they are secure. Check the skis; look for cracks or breaks. You

> ### Altitude Simulation Houses
>
> Cross-country skiers have used altitude simulation houses for several years to help them get used to training in the thinner (containing less oxygen) mountain air. Many top European and North American athletes use this technology to help them perform better. Instead of traveling to the mountains to train in thin air, athletes use altitude simulation houses to acclimate to the lower oxygen levels in higher altitudes.

don't want to get stranded miles from a ski lodge or transportation because of a bad binding or broken ski. If you're not using waxless boards, be sure to have the right wax for the ski conditions so you don't work harder than you need to.

Preseason Workouts

Is "exercise" a foreign word to you? Preparing for cross-country skiing by conditioning your body for a few weeks (longer is even better) before you begin can enhance the whole experience. Just like runners or cyclists, skiers need to build up their endurance and strength gradually.

Warming up is important whether you are going to ski across the backyard or go for a full marathon. Muscles and joints work much better when they are warmed up, stretched, and pumped. Warming up also prevents injury. Always stretch before you do any type of exercise. After you stretch, do a few exercises like sit-ups and push-ups, then move outside and do more sit-ups and push-ups.

Instead of starting out hard, begin skiing slowly. As you train, ease on up to racing and marathons by slowly increasing your speed and the length of your trail. Remember, your goal is to have fun, not miss ski season because of a preventable injury.

Fuel Up for the Boards

Fueling up is important since marathon skiing is an endurance sport. Running out of energy after a couple of miles out on the trail can make your ultra high-tech, lightweight skis feel like heavy planks of wood. The physical stress that results when a body is underfueled can cause you to fall or even ski out of control and hit a tree! Eating a healthy breakfast before a morning ski is key to a good day. Oatmeal, juice, and fruit are good body fuels. The day before a long XC ski is a good time to load up on carbohydrates. Whole

Poor nutrition and a lack of proper rest can make you exhausted.

grain bread, pasta with vegetables, and brown rice build energy. Save the meat and eggs for the day after your ski. They contain proteins that help repair tired muscles.

Water is important, too. All active people should drink eight eight-ounce glasses of water every day. Muscles need water to work properly during exercise. Skiers can become dehydrated competing in a race. During a race, drink a half cup of water every fifteen minutes to maintain proper hydration.

Catch Enough Zs

You'll be a slug out on the trail if you haven't had enough sleep. Eight hours is a good average for most people. If you're eating well and are in good physical condition you should have a good day on your boards. But if you are tired before you start or don't have the energy for even a slow burn out on the trail, chances are you're not getting enough sleep. Increase your sleeping time by half an hour and see if that helps.

Etiquette

Being considerate of other skiers on the slopes or trails can also help you stay safe. As a skier it's your responsibility to learn how to control yourself. During skiing lessons you can learn how to safely ski down trail hills, how to ski slowly, and how to come to a stop—without using other skiers as your personal pillow. If you're zipping along in a fine burn and another skier is crawling along in front of you, refrain from plowing by that person as you pass. Instead, call "Trail, please," and give the other skier a chance to step aside.

Pass other skiers politely to avoid collisions.

Winter Hazards

The longer and farther you intend to ski, the more prepared you need to be. If you plan to go out and tour the backcountry, carry a backpack. Fill it with extra clothes, food, a blanket, and a first-aid kit. A sudden snowstorm, injury, or avalanche can delay your return. If you're stuck outdoors overnight, the cold could freeze your skin (frostbite), uncovered fingers, toes, and ears. Your body temperature could also drop below 98.6 degrees, causing hypothermia. Knowing how to prevent and treat frostbite and hypothermia can make your skiing experience even better. You might think about taking a first-aid class. Ask a ski center or your ski instructor for information on first-aid classes.

4 Cross-Country Gear

When you realize you are hooked on XC skiing you will probably want to buy your own equipment. Shop around for good deals and high-quality gear. Ski clubs often have ski swaps. Members bring in used gear and trade with others. Package deals that combine skis, poles, boots, and bindings at mega-sports stores in shopping malls may be appealing, but be sure that the equipment is well made. Also, employees at larger sports outlets might not know as much as those at a store that specializes in ski equipment.

Before you buy be sure to borrow or rent as much equipment as you can until you find exactly what you want. As your skills grow and you decide to try backcountry, telemarking, or racing, you'll want to buy new skis every few years to take advantage of the latest advances in ski technology.

In addition to the long, skinny classic skis used in cross-country touring and racing, the skis used for skating, or freestyle, are fatter and shorter. Both of these ski types are used in marathon races. The skis used for telemark skiing, or telemarking, look much like Alpine skis. High-tech materials are used to make skis specifically suited to every style and technique, varying snow conditions, and the individual needs of skiers.

A cross-country skier leaves a winding trail through the snow as she telemarks down a slope.

In the past, classic cross-country boots used to look like a dull pair of shoes. Today, the high-tech boots used in racing are made for the best performance. Boots for backcountry or expedition skiing are also high tech and look like hiking boots. The heel of the cross-country boot is loose so you can skate and ski uphill, as well as use the telemark technique for going downhill.

Ski Styles and Fit

Due to the variety of cross-country ski techniques and events, there are several different styles of cross-country skis. Classic skis are the skinniest skis in this sport. These are also the same type of skis used for ultra skiing races. Racing skis are an extremely high-tech type of classic ski and can be expensive.

Classic skis are typically used for classic-style cross-country skiing in the human-made tracks of groomed trails. Cross-country skis are made of a variety of materials. A ski might have a wood core and be coated in plastic at the base (the surface that touches the snow). Your skis might also be constructed of carbon, graphite, Nomex (a strong and flexible plastic fiber), and foam. These materials help make today's skis lightweight, fast, stable, and comfortable.

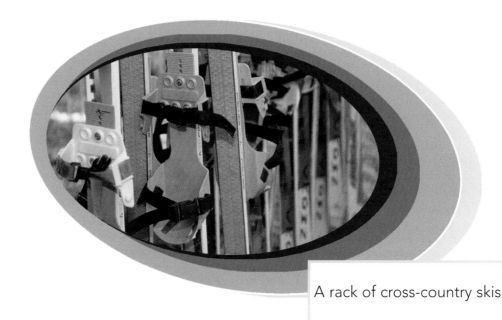

A rack of cross-country skis

Skating skis are a little shorter than classics. They have finished edges to help skaters rip along the trails with good grip and push, and turn or stop more quickly. Skiers also step out of the groomed trails to take their classics into areas that are not groomed. Backcountry skis are a little wider and shorter than classics. They are made for rugged deep-woods skiing and the unexpected downhills of unmarked territory.

Skis used specifically for telemark skiing very much resemble those used in Alpine skiing. But like all cross-country skis, the heel of the boot is not attached to the ski. Telemark skis work well on the groomed slopes shared with Alpine skiers.

It's very important that your skis fit. When considering fit, the characteristics of the ski and the skier should be matched to enhance ski performance and enjoyment. How much bend a ski has, its length, binding position, and glide ability all affect its performance. How much you weigh, what kind of trail you'll ski on, and the snow conditions you will ski in determine which ski is best for you. A ski sales professional can help you choose the equipment best suited for you.

Wax

Wax, wax, wax! You hear a lot about wax in cross-country skiing. Wax allows you to glide and enables you to "kick" so that you can easily slide into a glide. Wax also provides you with the grip needed to skate or ski up hills. Waxed skis are easier to control, and more control means better and safer downhills and turns.

There are a variety of waxes on the market. Each performs in a different temperature range and snow condition. Each manufacturer

Nat Brown, a former wax technician for the U.S. Olympic cross-country ski team, tunes a ski at his workshop in Edmonds, Washington.

has its own line and recommendations. If you're a beginner, so much information and so many choices can be pretty intimidating. A cross-country ski shop employee or a ski instructor can help you learn more about waxing.

There are also waxless skis. Waxless skis have patterns carved onto their bottoms below your boot placement to provide grip during uphill skiing. Waxless skis are convenient if you're a beginner. You won't be able to ski quite as fast with them as you would with properly waxed skis, but beginners and casual athletes won't notice the difference.

Boots

Boots for cross-country skiing are constructed to support the foot and ankle, but are not large and stiff like Alpine ski boots. Get a good fit in your XC boots. If they're too big they'll be unstable. If they're too small, you'll have cold, painful feet. Backcountry ski boots look like hiking boots.

Smart Clothes

When it comes to cross-country ski race clothing, thinner is better. Because it's an endurance sport, you're going to become an energy-burning machine out on the trails. If you become too hot from many layers of clothes you'll exhaust yourself. Avoid bulky clothes, as they can get in your way and restrict movement.

Try layering your clothing so that as you heat up you can remove layers and then put them back on again as you cool down. The old standby used to be thin cotton layers next to your skin, and wool on the outside. But now there are high-tech microfiber fabrics that work much more efficiently. They are thin and lightweight, yet keep you warmer and dryer.

Most beginners don't happen to have high-tech clothing on hand unless they've also been involved in other winter sports, like downhill skiing or snowboarding. So a good beginner's ski outfit might be polypropylene (synthetic fiber) long underwear, synthetic fleece (like Polartec) pants and shirt, and wind-resistant pants and jacket. Parkas and ski bibs or pants used for Alpine skiing are too bulky and retain too much body heat—you'll soon feel like you're roasting in an oven if you try to ski cross-country in them.

High-tech microfiber fabrics allow skiers to dress lightly, yet stay warm.

During your first ski outings, layer your clothes. The goal is comfort and the ability to move freely. Don't forget to wear a hat and gloves. Layering your socks is a good idea, too. Sweat is wicked (pulled) away from your feet so they won't get cold. You can wear a thin sock or a thick sock. Most people have a preference. Just make sure a thick sock will not make your boot fit too tightly.

Poles

Every pole will have a grip on top and a "basket" near the pointed bottom. The basket is a plastic disc that stops the pole from going deep into the snow. Poles come in a variety of materials, lengths, and grip styles. For example, you might want fiberglass poles with a big basket for rugged backcountry skiing. But for racing, you'll probably want to use lightweight carbon fiber poles with a cork grip and straps that fit snugly around your wrists. Skiers should make sure that their poles are the correct length and style. If poles are too long or too short, they can strain a skier's back and tire his or her arms. The correct pole length is determined by your height. A good rule of thumb is to shop for poles that stand as high as your armpits. This size lets you reach forward to plant and push backward with more power.

Bindings

Bindings attach the boot to the ski. Different binding styles suit different skis and skiing techniques. Where the binding is mounted on the ski can affect performance. For beginners, this isn't that important. But for elite cross-country athletes, the drag, or resistance, created by the binding can mean the difference between a win and a loss.

It's pretty easy to start skiing cross-country: Strap on the skis and start striding and gliding. It's the endurance part of the marathon or ultra races that can be exhausting. But if you work your way up to a marathon gradually, you will build up your strength and learn the skills you need to become an ultra skier.

As you train, pay close attention to your technique. Successful marathon skiing involves using physical energy efficiently so that you can keep going strong. Unnecessary movements can slow you down and needlessly waste the energy you so desperately need to make it to the finish line.

Moving the Boards

If you're interested in becoming a classic cross-country skier, you will most likely start skiing using the walking stride. Typically when you walk, as you put one foot forward, you swing the opposite arm forward too. Similarly, on skis, as you stride, if you slide one foot forward on its ski, your opposite arm should come forward. The trick is to stay relaxed and allow your body to move naturally.

Using the Poles

Learning how to use the poles is important, too. It looks easy when you see professional skiers using them. That's because they've got lots of experience and know how to move smoothly and gracefully.

Poles help skiers maintain balance, and push them forward. As a skier moves forward he or she plants the pole into the snow and pushes down and back. This gives forward thrust.

Straps are attached to the tops of the poles and circle the wrists; they help keep the poles in a skier's hands. Without straps it's easy to drop poles.

Knowing how to use poles correctly can add power to your glide and help you use your body's energy more efficiently. While beginners tend to alternate the

Experienced skiers treat their poles as extensions of their arms.

swinging of their arms and consequently push off only one pole at a time into the snow, experienced skiers use the double-pole technique. Double poling is a technique wherein a skier uses both poles at the same time to push forward.

Carving into Turns

While cross-country skiing takes place mostly on flat or gently rolling terrain, every now and then you're going to face a hill. It may not be a very high hill, but if it causes you to have the tips (front) of your skis lower than the tails (back), you're going to need to learn how to turn or stop. Once you do, you'll be carving (turning) in no time.

Learning how to turn is the first step toward skiing downhill. Also, if you're going to be on slippery surfaces, you're going to fall. Everyone does sooner or later. If you don't do it on the flats, you'll certainly do so sometimes on the downhills. In fact, most XC injuries happen on downhills. You'll want to be able to control your speed and stop when moving downhill. All beginners in Nordic and Alpine skiing learn a basic braking technique known as snowplowing. To snowplow, skiers bend their knees forward and bring them together. At the same time, they point their toes inward and push out gently with their heels. This technique forms the skis into a wedge, or the shape of a snowplow. The inside edges of the snowplow wedge push against the snow and slow the skier's speed. The degree of bend in the knees, toes, and heels controls the speed on a downhill.

The next step is to turn. Turning is a matter of shifting weight. Skiers lean slightly left in the plow to turn left. A slow right lean

You are almost sure to encounter a
few hills while cross-country skiing.

turns a skier's direction to the right. Practicing the snowplow on an open groomed downhill will make you an expert quickly.

The trick to falling is to do so without injury. The easiest, cleanest way to fall is backward, planting your butt in the snow. If you fall forward, don't use your hands to cushion the fall as you might break your wrists. Instead, tuck your elbows in and let your forearms hit the snow.

You'll need to learn how to get yourself back up on your skis once you do fall. After you unwind your skis and legs, turn around on your side so that your skis are downhill from you and pointed across the hill rather than up and down. Roll onto your hip, dig into the snow with the lowest ski, and come up on your uphill knee. Push with your hands and stand up on the downhill ski. Don't use your poles—you may bend or break them.

Special Training

How long does a good racer ski in a typical fifteen-kilometer course? Forty-five minutes. A breakdown of this time on the course might be fifteen minutes on the flats, five minutes on downhills, and twenty-five minutes on climbs. If you take racing seriously, PSIA recommends that you make training a daily routine. But don't try to squeeze all that training into your very first year. PSIA notes that the amount of training should be increased each year, over several years.

Roller Skiing

Serious racers, anxious to ski in warmer weather, use roller skis for non-snow training. Roller skis can be as expensive as regular skis, but they're high tech! They're three-feet long and can have air-filled tires, speed reducers, adjustable air pressure, shock systems that absorb some of the bumps in the road, and brakes. Roller skis allow racers to keep their competitive edge and enable anyone to gear up for snow season. Use older, cheaper poles for roller skiing—the pavement can be pretty tough on them. You can buy special tips for your poles if you're going to roller ski.

Training with roller skis does pose some risks—cars and obstacles in the road can cause accidents. And without the snow to cushion falls, injuries can be more serious. Always wear protective gear, including a helmet, when you plan to ski the roads. It's best to start roller skiing with a coach or other experienced roller ski athletes.

A skier struggles as she trains for the winter season on roller skis.

Once you've learned to cross-country ski you may find yourself wanting to check out the competition. Racing is a fun and exciting way to test yourself, your gear, and your training. It may seem like skiers race against each other, but out on the slopes you're really racing against the clock as you try to ski to a top finish time.

Local club races are a fine way to get started. You may enjoy the thrill of racing so much that you keep training and competing until you become an elite marathon XC skier.

Training Together

If you like to compete and enjoy the fun
and excitement of training

> ## What's a Marathon?
> A marathon can be anything that tests your physical endurance. In cross-country skiing it's a race, 50 kilometers or longer. The world's longest XC race is the 90k Vasaloppet held in Mora, Sweden.

for a race, that's all you need to begin racing. But if you want to become an elite XC athlete you'll need to train hard and well, and to do so, it helps to train with an experienced XC racer or coach.

You might think about joining an XC ski club. You can get together with other Nordic skiers and go out on group training runs. Clubs usually hold races for their members and often invite other clubs or nonmembers to enter their races. If you live in snow country, or within a day's travel of it, your school may have a ski club. And if it doesn't, see if you can start one. Your community may also have a ski club.

Bill Koch League

The Bill Koch Youth Ski League (BKYSL) is named for silver-medal Olympian Bill Koch. It's an XC ski program for children ages six to thirteen. BKYSL promotes both recreational and competitive XC skiing and includes ski jumping. During ski season, league members work on their ski skills, play at ski activities, and have

Beckie Scott

Beckie Scott is one of the top North American women competing in any of the Nordic categories. She placed fifteenth overall in the 2000 World Cup, was first in the 2000 Canadian Nationals, seventh in the 2000 Oslo World Cup Sprint, seventh in the 2000 Stockholm World Cup Sprint, and first in the U.S. Nationals. She began skiing at the age of five, joined the Jackrabbit Ski League, and skied her first race at seven. Her goal is to continue her international progress on the World Cup circuit and stand on the Olympic podium for Canada. Beckie holds a string of wins and top placements in Nordic competition. She competed in the 1998 Olympics in Nagano, Japan, and will no doubt be a part of the 2002 Olympic winter games in Utah.

fun races. Members don't have to race, and many stay in the league to keep building ski skills and to be involved in the fun. But if members do want to race, they'll be coached in building skills, speed, and endurance.

In professional competition, you race not only the other skiers, but the clock as well.

Jackrabbit League

In Canada, the Jackrabbit Ski League functions much like the Bill Koch Youth Ski League does in the United States. It teaches children to ski and helps them to develop their ski skills. If they wish to compete later, they can receive training for racing. The program has several age groups and functions, including the Bunnyrabbit program for ages four to seven and the Jackrabbit program for ages eight to thirteen. Also, the Racing Rabbits program for ages nine to fourteen introduces kids to racing, and the Challenge program for ages twelve and up continues development and

Skiers break from the gate at the beginning of the fifteenth annual Sons of Norway Barnebirkie race on February 22, 2001.

involvement in cross-country skiing. The league is named for Hermann "Jackrabbit" Smith-Johanssen, the man responsible for developing Canadian cross-country skiing. He skied until he was 107 years old.

The Pros

As you build your skills and gain experience in competition, you may want to compete on a higher level. Junior races are separated by age classes. There is also the Junior Olympics.

Your high school may have ski teams that compete with other schools. Once you reach your twenties you'll race with adults and in races open to all age groups. There are two types of races: citizen and classified.

Citizen races are open to anyone of any age and ability. These races are fun social events, but plenty of serious racers compete in them. You can find plenty of competition in citizen races. Citizen races are considered a Class II event by the United States Ski Association (USSA).

In classified races, racers must belong to one of the national or international race organizations endorsed by the International Federation de Ski (FIS). The USSA Competition Division is the national organization of the FIS. It keeps track of point standings for all racers. These races are considered Class I.

Where to Race

Youth ski races are a great way to start competing. Two major races in the United States sponsored by the American Ski Marathon Series (ASM) are the American Birkebeiner in Hayward, Wisconsin, and the Mora Vasaloppet held in Mora, Minnesota. ASM began in 1978 as the Great American Ski Chase. Today, the ASM organizes races for all levels of XC skiers.

At the American Birkebeiner there are two races for children. The Barnebirkie is a race held for children ages three to thirteen. The focus is on fun rather than competition. Racers can ski for 1k, 2.5k, or 5k. The Junior Birkie is a race for children ages ten to fifteen. It is an intermediate race for youth skiers. The distance is

Marathon cross-country skiing is challenging, but it is also a lot of fun.

2.5k, the same distance as the Junior Olympic qualifying races. At the Mora Vasaloppet, the Miniloppet is held for children up to thirteen years old in 1.5k, 4k, and 7k courses.

Now that you know all about cross-country skiing, are you ready to give it a try? Get some skis, find some snow, find a club, join a league, and enter a race. The Birkie, loppets, and Olympics could be in your future. Skiers, mount your boards and begin the burn!

Glossary

Alpine skiing Downhill skiing where chairlifts are used to get up the mountain.

backcountry skiing Skiing in the woods and mountains away from groomed trails.

biathlon Competition that combines events in rifle shooting and cross-country skiing.

citizen races Informal Nordic races for the public, open to all skiers.

classic technique The diagonal stride technique using kick and glide.

double pole Movement that uses both poles to move forward on skis.

glide zone The tips and tails of the ski base.

groomed trails Machine-prepared tracks and skating lanes.

hot waxing Ironing the glide wax into the base of a ski.

kick Stepping down on the ski to get a grip on the snow.

kick wax Temperature-graded wax used in the kick zone of the ski for grip.

kick zone The section of the ski base under the foot.

linked turns Moving from one turn into another without stopping.

marathon Any ski race that is fifty kilometers or longer.

Nordic combined A competition that includes the events of cross-country racing and ski jumping.

skating Using Nordic skis to skate on snow.

snowplow Using the braking wedge position to slow or stop your descent down a slope.

stride A forward step in cross-country skiing.

telemark A specific style of downhill skiing where one ski trails the other and turns are led with the outside ski.

touring Skiing on and off groomed trails.

touring center Ski area with groomed and marked trails.

waxless skis Skis with a pattern cut into the kick zone for grip.

Ultra Info

Bill Koch Youth Ski League
c/o New England Nordic Ski Association
23 Fletcher Road
Fairfax, VT 05454
(802) 849-2270
Web site: http://www.nensa.net

Professional Ski Instructors of America
133 South Van Gordon Street, Suite 101
Lakewood, CO 80228-1703
(303) 987-2700
e-mail: psia@psia.org
Web site: http://www.psia.org

United States Olympic Committee
National Headquarters
One Olympic Plaza
Colorado Springs, CO 80909
(719) 632-5551
Web site: http://www.usoc.org

United States Ski and Snowboard Association (USSA)
Box 100
1500 Kearns Boulevard
Park City, UT 84060
(435) 649-9090
Web site: http://www.ussa.org

In Canada

Canadian Freestyle Ski Association
2197 Riverside Drive, Suite 305
Ottawa, ON K1H 7X3
(613) 526-0551

Cross Country Canada
c/o Jackrabbit Ski League
1995 Olympic Way, Suite 100
Canmore, AL T1W 2T6
e-mail: cccanada@telusplanet.net
Web site: http://canada.x-c.com

Web Sites

American Birkebeiner Ski Federation
http://www.birkie.com

Cross Country Canada
http://canada.x-c.com

Cross Country Ski Areas Association
http://www.xcski.org

Cross Country Ski Northwest Wisconsin
http://www.norwiski.com

Cross-Country Ski Online
http://www.cross-countryski.com

Eagle River Nordic
http://www.ernordic.com
ER does extensive research on XC gear and skier performance

Gallatin National Forest Avalanche Center
http://www.mtavalanche.com
Includes avalanche education

Go Ski
http://www.goski.com
Find ski resorts throughout the United States and the world

Trailsource Cross Country Skiing
http://www.trailsource.com/xcs
Find trails anywhere

United States Ski Team
http://www.usskiteam.com

United States Telemark Ski Association of America
http://www.ustsa.org

Worldloppet Ski Federation
http://www.worldloppet.com

xcskiworld.com
http://www.xcskiworld.com

Ultra Reading

Books

Cazeneuve, Brian. *Cross-Country Skiing—A Complete Guide*. New York: W.W. Norton, 1995.

Gullion, Laurie. *Nordic Skiing: Steps to Success*. Champaign, IL: Human Kinetics, 1992.

Moynier, John. *Avalanche Aware* (Falcon Guide). Helena, MT: Falcon Publishing Company, 1998.

Moynier, John. *Cross-Country Skiing* (Basic Essentials Series). Guilford, CT: Globe Pequot Press, 1999.

O'Bannon, Allen, and Mik Clelland. *Allen and Mike's Really Cool Backcountry Ski Book: Traveling and Camping Skills for a Winter Environment*. Helena, MT: Falcon Publishing Company, 1996.

Parker, Paul. *Free-Heel Skiing*. Seattle, WA: Mountaineers Books, 1995.

Wiesel, Jonathan, and Dianna Delling. *Cross-Country Ski Vacations: A Guide to the Best Resorts, Lodges, and Groomed Trails in North America*. Santa Fe, NM: John Muir Publications, 1999.

Video and CD-ROM

(CD-ROM) *The Tao of Skiing* by Lisa Meloche, David McMahon. XCZONE Films, 1999.

(Video) *Nordicross!* by Dan Clausen. Anderson Video
    Communications, 1988.

Magazines

Couloir
P.O. Box 2349
Truckee, CA 96160
(530) 582-1884
email: couloir@telis.org
Web site: http://www.couloir-mag.com

Cross Country Skier
P.O. Box 83666
Stillwater, MN 55083-0666
(800) 827-0607
Web site: http://www.crosscountryskier.com

Powder
P.O. Box 58144
Boulder, CO 80322
(800) 289-8983
Web site: http://www.powdermag.com

Ski
P.O. Box 55533
Boulder, CO 80322
(800) 678-0817
Web site: http://www.www.skimag.com

Ski Canada
35 Riviera Drive, Bldg. 17
Markham, ON L3R 8N4
Canada
(800) 263-5295
Web site: http://www.skicanadamag.com

Ski Racing (e-zine)
Web site: http://www.skiracing.com

Index

A

alpine/downhill skiing, 6, 7, 12,
    13, 31, 33, 35, 40
altitude simulation house, 26
American Birkebeiner, 49
American Ski Marathon (ASM), 49

B

backcountry skiing, 24, 29, 31, 33
Bill Koch Youth Ski League,
    45–46, 47
bindings, 20–21, 25, 26, 33, 37
Birkebeiners, 11
Birkebeiner ski races, 11, 15, 49
boots, 20–21, 31–32, 33, 35, 37

C

Canadian Association of Nordic
    Ski Instructors (CANSI), 20, 25
carving, 40
citizen races, 49
classic style, 7, 21, 32, 38
classified races, 49
clothing, 9, 21, 35–36
competition, 14–16

cross–country skiing
history of, 5, 6, 9, 10–12, 14, 16
styles of, 7
technique, 17, 38–42
where to go, 7, 9, 17–18, 22–23

E

equipment/gear, 7, 9, 20–22,
    25–26, 30–37, 43
buying, 22, 30–31
renting, 21–22, 25, 31
etiquette, skiing, 28

F

face plant, 19, 24
falling, 42
freestyle, 7, 23, 31, 33

H

Hakonsson, King Hakon, IV, 11, 15

I

injury, 17, 19, 24, 27, 29, 40, 42
International Federation de Ski
    (FIS), 49

J

Jackrabbit Ski League, 46, 47–48
Junior Olympics, 48, 49
Junior World Championship, 15

K

Koch, Bill, 9, 16, 45

L

lessons, 18–20, 24–25, 28
loppet, 14–15
Loppet World Cup, 16

M

Mora Vasaloppet, 49

N

National Ski Association of
    America, 14
nordic skiing, 6, 9, 23, 40, 45, 46
Nordic World Ski Championships,
    15–16
nutrition, 27–28

O

Olympics, 9, 16, 46

P

poles, 7, 19, 36–37, 39–40, 43
Professional Ski Instructors of
    America (PSIA), 20, 25, 42

R

races/marathons, 5, 7, 8–9, 16,
    17, 26, 31, 32, 37, 44–45,
    46, 47, 48–49, 51
    training for, 44–45
    types of, 49
roller skiing, 42–43

S

safety, 24–29
Scandinavia, 6, 10–12, 15
Scott, Beckie, 46
skijouring, 20
ski clubs, 7, 14, 23, 30, 44, 45, 51
ski lift, 6, 12, 13, 19
ski resorts, 7, 18, 21–22, 23, 26
skis, 7, 19, 21, 31, 33
    types of, 21, 32–33
ski skating, 7, 23, 31, 33
sleep/proper rest, 28
Smith-Johanssen, Hermann
    "Jackrabbit," 48
snowboarding, 7, 35
snowplowing, 40, 42
snowshoes, ancient, 12
stopping, 28, 40

T

telemarking, 13, 31, 32, 33
terminology, ski, 19
Thorensen, John (Snowshoe
    Thompson), 14

trails, 7, 22–23, 24, 27, 28, 32, 33
training, 42
turning/turns, 40–42
  linking, 13

U

ultra sports, definition of, 5
Union Pacific Railroad Company, 12
United States Ski Association, 49

W

warming up, 26–27
wax, 21, 33–34
waxless skis, 21, 26, 34
winter hazards, 29
workout, preseason, 26–27
World Cup, 15, 16, 46

Credits

About the Author

Sandy Stiefer is a freelance writer who has been involved in sports and the outdoors her entire life. Her favorite winter sport is mushing with her six Siberian huskies. She writes for children and adults about health, gardening, animals, and sports. She lives near Kansas City, Missouri.

Photo Credits

Layout and Design

Thomas Forget